stoic.

/ˈstəʊɪk/

noun

a person who can endure pain or hardship without showing their feelings or complaining.

an anthology of poems

sabhyata ravjani

PAPER TOWNS
PUBLISHERS

First Published by
Paper Towns Publishers
72, Vishwanath Dham Colony,
Niwaru Road, Jhotwara,
Jaipur, 302012

Stoic

ISBN Print Book - 978-81-19455-75-1

Printed in India

"To live is the rarest thing in the world. Most people exist, that is all."

-oscar wilde

author's note

i've always had a flair for writing, but i never thought i'd be publishing my own book, especially at the age of 14. over the past few years, my emotions have taken me on quite a journey. i've felt substantially, but also, there were moments when i felt lost, as if a deep void consumed me. instead of dwelling on the events that transpired, i found an alternative means to express my sentiments, be it desolation, loneliness, or sorrow. of course, writing has consistently served as a way to stabilize my disarray of a mind.

the reason for this was twofold. A: there were instances when i had no one to confide in, no one capable of truly grasping the profound depths of my emotions, which often took a considerable effort for even me to comprehend. B: some people whom i considered my friends, went as far as to go ahead and say that i "overreact" to every little thing. now, what was left was me, with my diary. so, i turned to poetry to articulate my innermost thoughts and emotions.

primarily, my aim was self-expression, an endeavour to confront my feelings more eloquently. however, a greater purpose soon became clear. i realized i wanted my work to touch the lives of many. i was aware that i was not alone in this journey, that countless individuals battle mental health issues every single day. most of them, perhaps, are overwhelmed, feeling alienated and frightened. my aspiration is to assure them that they are not alone and that we share a connection.

here's to flipping the middle finger to those who belittle your struggles and claim that you merely "overreact." i want you to know that every emotion you experience is valid, and together, we can transcend the stigma surrounding mental health.

whether or not you find yourself in these words, here's to a journey we're embarking upon together. if you do, i empathize and thank you – for we share a connection, and you're not alone. and if you don't, cheers to exploring new perspectives and stories. let's begin this journey together.

— S.R.

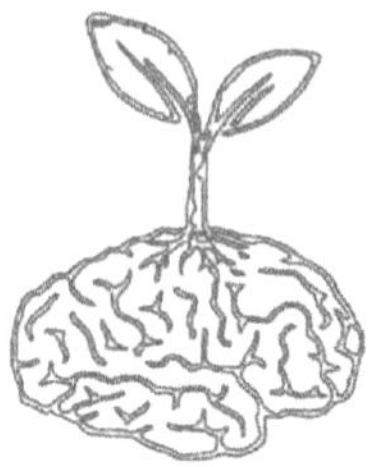

don't we all have to grow?

DATE 10 / 03 / 23

i think, if i shared half my problems, i'd be as happy as a clam,
even though i abhorred sham.
so i had to bottle up that pain,
but when it came to them, my fickle mind emerged into action again.
just when they said, i miss us,
i realized i'd wasted too much time on this fuss.
trying to make it something it never was.
whatever we had, it isn't the same anymore,
no matter how hard we try to mould.
it just won't be the same.
however, i try to be thankful for this.
it was 8 years ago,
but don't we all have to grow?

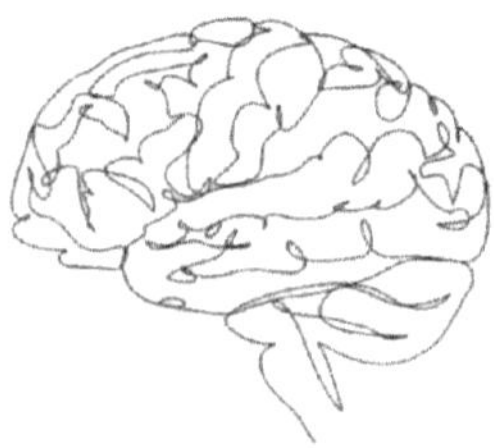

the mind

the pressure that gets to us all, at some point,
in order to meet the expectations and not disappoint,
we try our best to obtain the validation as you get to the checkpoint.
we let ourselves get dominated by the burden,
and let ourselves turn into someone else, a complete different person,
unknowingly, we create another sham version.
soon, we cannot bear it and tend to explode,
and finally cease what appeared to be excessive work mode.
without realizing what we've left behind,
without realizing that we've created a new machine called the mind.

flood of feelings

DATE 13 / 03 / 23

they don’t know what they took away from me,
i might be smiling,
but inside i’m dying
because i can’t bear it anymore
the flood of feelings, can't keep it in anymore.
they were ignored like the birds chirping in the morning,
what if i was young? despite, my feelings were too scorning,
for them to disregard.
as if it were just a materialistic object to discard.
it had afflicted me,
since it was gone, i was just left there with the solitude to be.
it’s all interconnected, the emptiness, the sadness, the nostalgia.

unnerving insomnia

paralyzed but not literally,
trying to disregard my mind's peculiar imagery.
laying there was like resting in restlessness.
generating a feeling of helplessness.
staring at the ceiling,
couldn't put a name to this feeling.
but my thoughts were a web of nothing and everything at the same time.
waiting for my phone to chime,
and break the unnerving silence
it still bothered me, their absence.
the tick tock of the clock,
as it struck 3AM
a random thought reminded me of them.
who? i had no idea.
the unease was accompanied by insomnia.

how life goes on

DATE 05/04/23

i’ve started finding tranquility in the after hours,
when i’m the only one conscious.
trying to defeat my chronic insomnia,
i stare up at the ceiling every night.
hoping to not be a victim of sleep paralysis
as i look around at my disorganized surroundings.
can’t bear the crack of dawn,
as i try to fall asleep while others try to awake.
half the day goes by and i finally wake.
wondering how to utilize the remainder of the day.
and it's already night again.
on repeat: how life goes on.

DATE 21/04/23

i am a criminal.
although, not guilty yet.
so, close to them beating the truth out of me.
while i'm still a web of dead nerves,
that failed to fulfill their function.
as i sat there, feeling nothing.
my lips were a straight thin line,
likewise to the immobile skin suit i wore everyday.
the only operational organ, my eyes
who abandon me every second.
but, at least return to implement their purpose.
despite everything, i try to force the sentiment out.
as expected, it doesn't work
making me question everything,
am i even alive?

she was sad.
but after him
she smiled like she had finally forgotten her past.
she laughed so much as if she, too, was obsessed with the
new-found sound.
she cried but instead, tears of joy emerged down her eyes.
she knew her scars existed but learned to accept them.
she fell in love with the chirping of birds in the morning,
rather than the hoots of the owl at night.
she didn't need the sun to brighten up her days anymore.
after him, she wasn't fragile like a flower but refulgent like a
flower.
after him, she was strong like a thorn but not dead like a
thorn.

DATE 28 / 04 / 23

you wouldn't know
because i try not to reveal much.
if only you could see through the disguise.
do not stare too long in my eyes
i'm afraid you might recognise
the person who i was before it happened.
i'd rather swim with the sharks
to try and wash away those marks.
fighting an invisible battle
you see me but there's more to it
you wouldn't understand so let's just forget it.

intrusive thoughts

DATE 07/05/23

i wonder, will the day ever come
when i finally lose the battle
against my intrusive thoughts.
i clench my teeth and
clench my fists,
just thinking about my so-called enemies
makes me enraged and sick.
the littlest of things they do
to make me believe that they are the villains,
and not me, despite me letting
my intrusive thoughts win.

game of uno?

DATE 04/07/23

i keep trying so hard
to drop the reverse card
but it just keeps falling into a pit.
i rummage to find the skip card
but i feel lost in the fear of not winning.
the game is getting difficult
with players quitting on each level.
overthinking about what card to throw next,
i know this is all a test
but with no card left up my sleeve,
there's no other option but to leave.
what the future holds, who knows
in the end, it's just a game of UNO.

stifling expectations

DATE 21/07/23

my posture, starting to incline forward.
wonder if it's due to the constant,
indirect burden on my not-so fragile shoulders.
it feels impossible
to ever meet their expectations
expectations they expect from someone
who departed this life 3 years ago.
every night, at 3 AM, i conceive a plan
to survive without meeting the stifling expectations
that ought to linger for eternity.
although, i still hold some hope.
that one day it will all be enough.
after all, someday, we all have to escape the rat race
and end it for once and for all

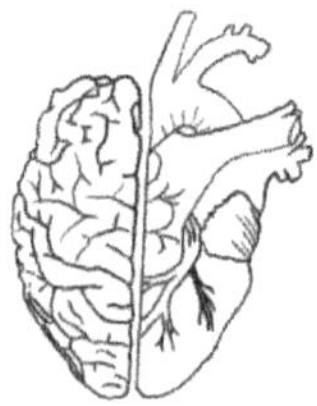

i have been so patient.
shit happened?
oh. no big deal, gotta get over it
happens with everyone
this is probably not the last time
but let's be hopeful, now, right?
and thank god for the good stuff
instead of whining about the bad stuff.
i have been so grateful.
shit happened again?
oh. no big deal, gotta get over it
it's nothing, worse has happened
you'll come around,
not a kid anymore, are we?
kids cry all the time
not adults like you.
stop. fucking. crying.
since when are you such a cry baby?
shut it. nobody's a fan of the dramatics.
quit moping around and wipe your tears
before someone notices something's wrong
which no one will, probably
but let's be hopeful, now, right?

DATE 12 / 10 / 23

i give
and i give
and i give more
for just a brief second i might even be proud of that,
but almost cleverly they don't let another second pass.
being the fool that i am,
i expect something in return; my only mistake.
even if it's solely asking for acknowledgement
or for my voice to be heard
they change colors to their original one
and in the snap of two fingers,
it's over.
such cowards, i wonder.
the people disgust me
whom i try so hard to hate
only to make me believe that
they lost me and not vice versa.

the other i

my mind is a complex paradox
pervaded with fake scenarios
and incidents that have transpired.
leaving me to question reality?
or...
have i acquired the ability to foresee my future?
scared. or maybe not.
my other i, who already anticipated it all.
emerges to gloat to my face.
"i told you so."
a devilish grin.
who do i believe?
i know she can hear this thought of bewilderment.
i know that she may be my better version;
something i aspire to be.
but also,
my other i, who sabotages my current self.
the negative voice in the back of my mind.
who do i believe?

new-found aspiration

a poem by sabhyata ravjani

wandered to various places.
yet, every place felt the same.
when i heard your soft voice, looked at your pretty eyes, all i saw was pain.
why? none of us knew. it was just there.
what was it that you desired?
was it the last stage of survival to finally be over?
to take your last breath,
for your body to finally rest?
you started to wonder.
why was this brutal world so cruel?
will i ever be free?
have i crossed the non-existent line?
i was held prisoner in my own mind,
by my own thoughts.
the feeling started to eat me alive.
nothing felt enough.
this unsettling emptiness.
never felt alive, something or everything was missing.
fed up with this life.
started to believe in the darkest hours of existence.
the only definition i knew was death.
waiting for my demise,
why wasn't it here yet?
were the grim-reapers too late?
finally, i closed my eyes.
"open them up again, what do you see?"
everything had changed.
aloof, detached, uninterested.
everything had changed.
i finally marked and initiated my goal.
to stop caring and take over the world.
i now believed in myself,
all that i could do in this world.
the drastic change was patent,
i started to believe in myself again.
believed that i couldn't leave this planet without making a difference.
stopped wondering why it was how it was.
a completely new person, was what i became.

14 poems at 14 years

before my 15th birthday approaches, i feel compelled to share these 14 poems, the result of a creative journey that commenced at the tender age of 14. it is my sincere wish that they provide solace to those who have suffered in silence.

additional message

as an additional message to those who battle self-harm, here are a few bonus templates that might help in tough times. remember that i stand with pride in your daily strength.

DATE/DAY:

why i feel like doing it today:
(you may use this space to scribble)

on a scale of 1- 10, how bad is it?

1 2 3 4 5 6 7 8 9

you're stronger than you know. every day you confront is a victory, showcasing your strength and resilience. you are not alone in this journey, and there is help and support available.

you are very strong.

DATE/DAY:

why i feel like doing it today:
(you may use this space to scribble)

on a scale of 1- 10, how bad is it?

① ② ③ ④ ⑤ ⑥ ⑦ ⑧ ⑨

you are worth the fight, and your journey is far from over. don't give up; brighter days await on the path to healing. reach out to someone you trust, because you are worth every effort to heal and find light again.

you are worth it.

DATE/DAY:

why i feel like doing it today:
(you may use this space to scribble)

on a scale of 1- 10, how bad is it?

(1) (2) (3) (4) (5) (6) (7) (8) (9)

i'm immensely proud of your journey and the distance you've traveled. your strength shines brightly; keep moving forward. count your good days instead of your bad.

i'm proud of you.

throughout the journey of writing this book, i've found myself wrestling with doubts. there were moments when i questioned whether sharing my thoughts, experiences, and vulnerabilities would open me up to judgment, perhaps from people i know or even from those i've never met. the act of laying bare my inner world in these pages left me feeling exposed, and i grappled with the fear of attracting the attention of many and the potential for criticism.

however, as i stand at the crossroads of completion, i have come to realize that what matters most is the possibility of making even the smallest impact on you, readers. it is with this realization that i release those apprehensions and embrace the pride of being the author of this book. in sharing this journey with you, i hope that you, too, feel a sense of pride as you hold these pages in your hands.

acknowledgements

in closing, i want to express my heartfelt gratitude to you, dear reader. your time and willingness to engage with the content of this book have not gone unnoticed. it is through your commitment to understanding and improving your mental health that the pages preceding this conclusion have found their purpose.

remember that healing is a journey, one that may be marked by twists and turns, but it is a journey you do not undertake alone. your courage in seeking understanding and support is commendable, and it's worth recognizing that each step you take toward a healthier mindset is a step in the right direction.

as you close this book and embark on the path of self-discovery and well-being, take with you the knowledge that you possess the strength to overcome obstacles, the resilience to face challenges, and the capacity to find joy in each day. your mental health is a precious part of your being, and it deserves care and attention.

with unwavering hope, i encourage you to continue seeking understanding, seeking help when needed, and, above all, seeking the beauty of a life that is yours to shape and cherish.

wishing you peace, resilience, and a future filled with well-being and contentment.

farewell,
sabhyata ravjani.